Iggle the Eagle
By Jonathan Hershman

For my grandfather. For the glory. For Philadelphia.

ISBN: 9798578028359

In a small city, on the east coast of the United States

Lies a town of unique people in an unusual space.

Not too far inland, yet a few hours from the shore

Is a place called Philadelphia, where eagles run and soar.

Over the streets of the city high above the art museum steps

Was born a little eagle named Iggle with a large heart booming in his little chest.

Boom, boom his heart would thump as he'd peak over his nest

At larger birds flying by fast, soaring from east then to west.

With little wings, little feathers, and little feet

He was much smaller than the other birds but smirked with ambitions from his little beak.

Every year in Philadelphia the largest, strongest Eagles would meet

To race in the skies of the city up, down, and over Broad Street.

The race goes from north to south over the statue of William Penn,

A cut through Elfreth's Alley and then in a bend

To follow the Schuylkill past the falls and toward the river's end,

And finally crossing the finish on the New Jersey side of the Walt Whitman.

Although little, Iggle the Eagle had bigger, stronger, and ambitious bird dreams

That would swell up his chest and make him burst at the seams.

Every day over Broad Street he'd watch large eagles fly farther and faster

Zooming uptown and downtown past the University schoolmasters.

Excited about the prospect of similarly soaring someday,

"I bet I'll fly farther and faster than all of them," he'd surely say.

"I will fly over the buildings and through the city just for the gritty city smell,

I'll go over the cars and head toward the Liberty Bell.

I'll go up and down and some days over the Walt Whit.

And perhaps do a couple loops around Reading Terminal Market.

As soon as all my feathers come in you will see

I'll be the fastest eagle ever to race in Philly."

All the other birds laughed at Iggle and said with a cry,

"Your wings are too small, your beak is too wide, and you wiggle your head side to side when you fly.

Those faster birds are born with stronger wings that are meant to go fast—

Much stronger features than yours—against them you won't last.

They were meant to fly high and zip through the skies, so naturally gifted they should win a prize.

You should dream of something different, more appropriate, for a bird of your size."

Iggle puffed out his chest and said with a grin, "There's something you should know, something I should mention..."

"Those 'gifted birds' feathers are brown, and their talons are long,

And their wingspan is wide, and their tails are quite strong.

Each of their beaks has a bright mustard yellow shine

Those birds were born with the same features as me, features that look just like mine.

If they can fly faster than lightning at the Franklin Institute

Then so can I, because I'm an eagle too"

So with his big dreams and a big puff in his small chest

Little Iggle went to bed with intentions to get lots of rest.

"I'll set my alarm early, to begin my training

I plan to fly several miles, even if it is raining.

Every day I'll have to work full and I'll have to work hard

And I'll get up early before traffic hits the Boulevard.

I may be small and my head wiggles when I fly

But none of that matters with the work I'll put in and how hard I will try."

And Iggle's alarm went off the next morning as he woke in a blur

"Ugh I'm too tired to fly, maybe I'll start tomorrow," he murmured in a purr.

He thought of reasons to start on another day, or maybe to start in some other way,

Reasons that he wasn't ready to practice, or should be like all birds of prey.

Then he looked in the mirror and squawked out loud,

"This dream is too important and I'm much too proud

To wait any longer for time to drift by

I'm Iggle the Eagle and I'm ready to fly."

And Iggle jumped off the ledge and began his wing flap

And he flapped as he went, and he flapped really fast

But he quickly grew tired and ran out of gas.

"I'll never be able to hold that pace, not one little bit,"

He said with a little whiff, "I'll never make it over the Walt Whit."

Looking for inspiration, he soared to Independence Hall

And read about the Founders who filled him with an immense Philly awe.

"In the face of uncertainty, brave men moved most certainly

Toward a lofty goal that was courageous and new.

And if they're capable of achieving large goals, then I surely can, too."

Every morning thereafter, Iggle took flight.

"Little by little I'll work hard and then even I might

Achieve my great goal or maybe I will fail

But with my little wings and my brave feathered tail

I won't leave it to chance, and I will surely try

I want to get better after every fly.

Some days I'll fly long and some days I'll fly fast

But doubting myself will be a thing of the past."

Other birds continued to look and to wonder why

And kept insisting that a small bird who was born undersized

Would never be able to beat the bigger birds in a bigger race

That went down Broad Street, across the bridge, never at their bigger pace.

"Iggle - you're entirely too small,

Not born with strong, wily wings like them all.

You can't fly like them—you'll simply just fall.

The other birds are born with talents that we've seen move so fast

Talents that you weren't born with and that you frankly lack."

Iggle was hurt but he remained strong

Because he believed in himself, and what they were saying was wrong

With a big puff in his little chest, he closed his little eyes

And took a big breath,

Flapped his wings, and politely squawked up a small squawk,

"Their wings are all brown, they waddle when they walk,

Their heads are all bald, and their feet dry as chalk.

They were born with Eagle features, features just like mine

I can do whatever they can do because they are Eagles and so am I."

In the weeks leading up to the really big race

Iggle flew every day at a different flight pace.

He'd go north on Walnut or south onto South

And even kept going when he was dry in the mouth.

Sometimes he'd fly out and other times out and just go

Sometimes he'd do a few loops around Boathouse Row.

Some days were easy, and some days were fast,

Some days he went early and some days half past

Midnight or when he could find the time.

The other birds couldn't see him, but to him that was fine.

"They'll see me on race day when the big race begins

And they'll see me first past the finish line because I'm determined to win."

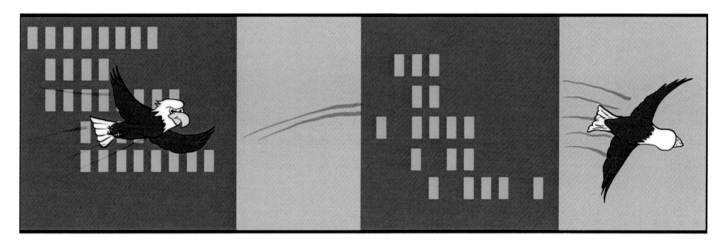

After weeks of buildup race day arrived

And surely Iggle lined up with birds that were one and a half times his size.

He took a deep breath and he slowly puffed.

He stretched out his wings and his wings slowly fluffed.

He went through his mantra and closed his bright eyes.

"If they can do it, then so can I.

Because we're ALL eagles, and I'm ready to fly!"

The race announcer yelled Go! and the big birds took off just like rockets

Iggle fell behind quickly as the others laughed like the race was in their pockets.

"It's a long race and I must refrain

From starting too fast, and trust how I trained."

The other birds whipped by as crowds rallied and scurried

They zoomed by Reading Terminal in an extreme racing hurry.

Iggle was in the back but never lost sight;

He wasn't going to give up, not this early in the fight!

He kept his eye on the leader and squinted like there was only something he knows

He felt good and said, "by the time they're at Pat's, I'll be at Geno's!"

The lead birds flapped past the old naval yard and began to grow tired

Iggle spotted this quickly and as quickly got fired

Up to finally make his move and he squawked a "Voilà!"

I'll catch them right before the stadiums and after the next Wawa.

Then little Iggle flapped his little wings and much to everyone's surprise

The little bird, not born with natural talents, and who was undersized

Moved out in front which was unbelievable to those who knew

Iggle's story, but at that very moment they remembered little Iggle was an eagle, too.

As he flew past the Linc, Iggle the Eagle was clearly the winner

And no one, but no one, would think he was a beginner.

As he suddenly realized he was going to win, he felt really smitten

That he was the smallest Eagle to be the first to cross the Walt Whitman.

The eagle mayor waddled to Iggle to raise up his wings

And said "In all my years I've praised many things.

But never have I seen with my own eagle eyes

A bird to win this race of Iggle's size.

For your inspiring efforts and determination never to settle

I award you our first place prize - a lifetime of glory and one soft pretzel!"

As Iggle looked around, the mood gently shifted

A reporter immediately asked him "How a little bird who wasn't naturally gifted

Flew so beautifully amongst bigger birds in order to win."

Iggle purred politely, "Where do I begin --

He thought for a second, looked up and looked down

Said, "Their claws are yellow, their legs are brown

Their talons are long and go down to the ground.

Every eagle is born with these traits and so am I,

Regardless of size every eagle can fly.

Perhaps the only thing in this race

Was that I could capture the heart of this special place.

When they say "Philly Special" they mean more than just a play

Because the spirit of this city grows bigger each day.

No dreams are too big, no opponents too strong

And that anyone is capable of proving doubters so wrong."

Iggle then took a bite of his pretzel and flew off with his lifetime of glory

But the best prize he won that day was the ability to tell his Iggle the Eagle story.

Made in United States
North Haven, CT
30 September 2023

42205322R00018